This
Ladybird Picture Book
belongs to

....

Ladybird Picture Books

Look out for...

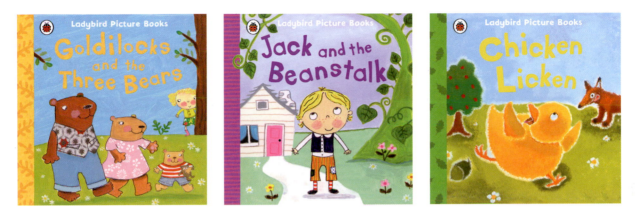

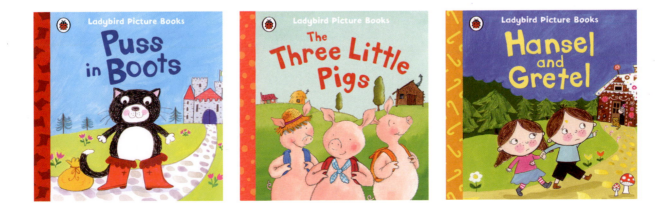

The turnip's so good that they can't get their fill
and it's just so ENORMOUS they're eating it still!

Then it was turnip for breakfast and lunch and for tea, and turnip for supper and… oh, deary me!

Anyone for seconds?

bump...
bump!

Miaow!

…the ENORMOUS turnip shot right out with a *THUD!* and a *THWACK!* and a *THUMP!* And they all fell back, with a…

Bump…

Whoops!

Ouch!

The man pulled the turnip, the wife pulled the man, the boy pulled the wife, the girl pulled the boy, the dog pulled the girl, the cat pulled the dog, the mouse pulled the cat and...

Squeak!

"Come and help heave!" called the cat to a mouse.

The man pulled the turnip, the wife pulled the man, the boy pulled the wife, the girl pulled the boy, the dog pulled the girl, the cat pulled the dog.

Miaow!

But the ENORMOUS turnip just wouldn't budge!

"Come and help heave!" called the dog to a cat.

But the ENORMOUS turnip just wouldn't budge!

Woof!

"Come and help heave!" called the girl to a dog.

The man pulled the turnip, the wife pulled the man, the boy pulled the wife, the girl pulled the boy, the dog pulled the girl.

But the ENORMOUS turnip just wouldn't budge!

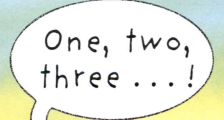

One, two, three . . . !

"Come and help heave!" called the boy to a girl.

The man pulled the turnip, the wife pulled the man, the boy pulled the wife, the girl pulled the boy.

But the ENORMOUS turnip just wouldn't budge!

"Come and help heave!" called the wife to a boy.

The man pulled the turnip, the wife pulled the man, the boy pulled the wife.

All together!

The man pulled the turnip and the wife pulled the man. But the ENORMOUS turnip just wouldn't budge!

Heave!

The man thought it must be time at last to pull the turnip, but it just stuck fast.

"Come and help heave!" called the man to his wife.

The man was baffled but he kept on hoeing.
And the ENORMOUS turnip kept on growing.

It grew bigger and bigger every day.
It was huge. It was vast. It was...

ENORMOUS!

The other poor turnips got out of its way.

One of the turnips – the best of the lot –
began to take over the whole of his plot.

Look at
that one!

At last the turnips began to grow. They got bigger and bigger and bigger.

And the man with the hoe said, "So... we'll have turnips for breakfast and lunch and for tea. And it's turnips for supper, too, thanks to me."

He plucked out the weeds and raked off the rubble.
He didn't know there was going to be trouble.

In a very few days came little green leaves. They poked and they pushed and they pointed. The man with the hoe rolled up his sleeves…

That's a weed!

He cared for his seeds and watered them well, and the turnip seeds began to...

swell...

Once, a man came out to his garden with his turnip seeds and his hoe. He dug and he delved and he set his seeds in a row.

Ladybird Picture Books

The
Enormous
Turnip

BASED ON A TRADITIONAL FOLK TALE

retold by Irene Yates ★ illustrated by Jan Lewis

LADYBIRD BOOKS

UK | USA | Canada | Ireland | Australia
India | New Zealand | South Africa
Ladybird Books is part of the Penguin Random House group of companies
whose addresses can be found at global.penguinrandomhouse.com.

www.penguin.co.uk　　　www.puffin.co.uk　　　www.ladybird.co.uk

First published 1999
Reissued 2012 as part of the Ladybird First Favourite Tales series
This Ladybird Picture Books edition published 2017
001

Copyright © Ladybird Books Ltd, 1999, 2012, 2017

Printed in China
A CIP catalogue record for this book is available from the British Library

ISBN: 978–0–241–31539–2

All correspondence to:
Ladybird Books, Penguin Random House Children's
80 Strand, London WC2R 0RL